George C. Adams

A Christian Lawyer

A sketch of the life and work of Hon. Warren Currier

George C. Adams

A Christian Lawyer
A sketch of the life and work of Hon. Warren Currier

ISBN/EAN: 9783337097752

Printed in Europe, USA, Canada, Australia, Japan

Cover: Foto ©Raphael Reischuk / pixelio.de

More available books at **www.hansebooks.com**

A CHRISTIAN LAWYER.

A SKETCH OF

THE LIFE AND WORK OF

HON. WARREN CURRIER,

BY

GEO. C. ADAMS, D.D.,

PASTOR COMPTON HILL CONGREGATIONAL CHURCH.
ST. LOUIS, MO.

ST. LOUIS:

COMMERCIAL PRINTING COMPANY.

1893.

PREFACE.

The reason for the frequent use of the word Congregationalism in this book is the utter impossibility of writing the story of this life without it. It is a part of his life, and he was one of those who have led it out into a larger life. The times have changed. That which fifty years ago meant to the world at large a New England sect is now a gospel of light and liberty to thousands who have felt the oppression of sect. For us provincialism is disappearing in nationalism. The horizon has widened, and at the same time the concentration of the life and thought of those who hold a common faith in fellowship that means aggressive work is having its effect. We are a denomination. We even dare to call ourselves a church. He whose life story is briefly told here stands for this change. Born and reared in New England, of the straitest sect; migrating to Missouri in the old South; there, like many others in similar circumstances, confessing the Savior, and entering actively upon church life; filling with great honor high positions both legal and mercantile, and thereby acquiring intimate knowledge of men and affairs; spending a part of many years in the old West, and the remainder in the new South; he represents in a marked degree the new and broad thought of Congregationalism, as a belief and polity, full of the Holy Spirit, wide as the globe, and united as the drops that form the ocean.

CONTENTS.

CHAPTER I.

THE STORY OF A LIFE.

Ancestry. Heroes of the Revolution. Influence of Christian Women. Childhood of Warren Currier. His Education. Value of Work. Admitted to the Bar. Marriage. Political Honors. Removal to St. Louis. In the Missouri Legislature. Revision of Statutes. Elected to the Supreme Bench of Missouri. Failing Health. Death of his Son Edward. Judge Currier's Religion. Joins the First Church, St. Louis. Origin of Pilgrim Church. His Part in It. His Jealousy for those Early Days. Call of Dr. Goodell. His Arrival in St. Louis. Welcomed to Judge Currier's Home. Letter from Mrs. Goodell. Pilgrim Church Anniversaries. Battle with Disease. The End of this Life.

CHAPTER II.

TRAITS OF CHARACTER.

Value of the Christian Lawyer. His Thoroughness. Shown in Childhood. Good Business Man. His Reading. Firm Convictions. Persistence. Value of these Qualities to his Church. Applauded Them in Others. Promptness. Excellent Judgment. Judicial Decisions. Notice in *Rocky Mountain Congregationalist*. Foresight in Church Matters. High Sense of Honor. Tribute to Gen. Lyon. Outspoken. Of Tender Heart. Interest in Young Men. Testimonies. An Optimist. His Faith. Views on Approaching Death. To His Grandchildren. Summary.

CHAPTER III.

HIS INFLUENCE ON THE CHURCH.

A Shaper of Events. Quiet Beneficence. Love for His Church. Interest in Home Missions. Church Work in the South. Denominational Aggressiveness. Quotations from his Writings. Care over Weak Churches. Origin of the National Council. He Introduces the Subject. Southern Association of Illinois. Report of Committee of Illinois State Association in 1867. Dr. J. E. Roy, in the *Congregationalist*. Judge Currier's Work in the Boston Council. Pilgrim Memorial Convention at Chicago in 1870. Letter to Dr. Patton. Interest in the Development of the Council. The Council a Working Body. His Article on It in the *Congregationalist*. His Longing for Christian Comity. Call for a Congress of Denominations.

CHAPTER IV.

HIS AID TO INDIVIDUAL CHURCHES.

A Useful Old Age. Planning to Do Good. A Practical Faith. "The National Council Exigency Loan Fund." Dr. Frisbie's Article. Judge Currier's Offer. Giving that Makes Others Give. Helping the Local Church. Giving Through Regular Channels. Incident of Biddle Market Mission. Third Church, St. Louis. Fifth. Central. Church of the Redeemer. Atlanta. Resolutions Passed by that Church. His Letter at the Dedication. Other Churches Aided by Him. Letter of Rev. A. Blanchard.

CHAPTER V.

HIS LEGAL SERVICES.

CHAPTER I.

THE STORY OF A LIFE.

"That man lives twice that lives the first life well."

—Herrick.

CHAPTER I.

THE STORY OF A LIFE.

It is the purpose of this sketch to place before the reader the life of a Christian lawyer; not that of a faultless man, but of one who, while at his daily work, found time to attend to the Lord's business, and who, when laid aside from active participation in the affairs of the day, was of great service in building up the visible Kingdom of God. A helpful Christian life is usually the result of some generations of careful training, and sturdy qualities do not appear by chance. A man's ancestry and his surroundings in childhood have much to do with his character, so it is well at the outset to speak of the birth-place and family.

The town records of Salisbury, now Amesbury, Mass., show that in 1640, twenty years after the landing of the Pilgrims at Plymouth, Richard Currier settled in Salisbury. He is regarded as the common ancestor of the now numerous family of New England Curriers It is not possible to trace the lineage directly from him to the present; but when the soldiers of the Revolution went forth to battle, among them was William Currier, a member of Captain Solomon Kidder's company in the regiment of Colonel Brooks. The imagination suggests a most interesting story of love and hardship in his case, as he was married in Billerica, Mass., to Betsy Richardson, a daughter of Ebenezer Richardson, by Rev. Henry Cummings, April 25th, 1775, only a week after the battle of Lexington. Whether he was one of the Billerica minute men, who turned out on that memorable occasion, and helped to make the retreat of the British a fight all the way to Charlestown Neck, we are not informed, but it is certain that shortly after that time he was in the ranks, and fought through the greater part of the war. He was the father of six children—five boys and one girl. The second son, Isaac, was born in Billerica, October 24th, 1777, made his home in Walpole, New Hampshire, and was the father of the subject of this sketch.

On the mother's side the record is equally honorable. She was a daughter of Joseph and Mary (Hearsy) Farnsworth. Her father was a soldier in the war of the Revolution, and drew a pension for many years after on account of services rendered at that time. His wife was a woman of rare excellence, and her earnest, consistent piety made a deep impression on her grandson, Warren, in his boyhood. He was more under her influence than that of his own mother, from whom he was much separated. Her example and teaching did more to give his mind a religious bias than all other external influences combined. It was another case of grandmother Lois and mother Eunice, and much of the sturdy character in the man was doubtless due to her teaching. She died while he was yet a lad. Her daughter, the mother of Warren Currier, inherited the good qualities of her mother. We have little of her history, but she left a vivid impression of love and good works upon the mind of her son.

In a letter which he wrote a year before his death, to one who bore her name, he says: "I say Lucy because I like that honored name; it was the name of my mother, who was not only a saint, but a woman of common sense, and read books. She died while I was yet very young. I remember the last time I saw her, and how I went away alone and wept very bitter tears. I was then but a lad, but the scene is all before me now, a hallowed remembrance. Many years after, and in mature manhood, as I passed that way, and came in sight of the same old hills, ' rock-ribbed and ancient as the sun,' the past reappeared before me in all its original impressive tenderness. I saw visions of angels and ministering spirits, and tears flowed again as in the early days of childhood. For the moment I was a child again, and the kingdom of heaven was all about me." This mother who, though separated from him, yet had such an influence on her child, died April 12th, 1834, greatly lamented by a large circle of acquaintance. Her husband had died nine years before, October 20th, 1825, and the widow, with six children and limited means of support, had seen her family scattered and away from her direct influence, in the effort to make a living.

Warren Currier was born in Walpole, New Hampshire, March 14th, 1817. The death of his father when he was eight, and that of his mother when he was seventeen years of age, would have thrown him upon the world early in life, to care for himself; but for some reason, not given, he was taken from their home when only about four years of age, and lived with an uncle till he was fourteen, when he struck out for himself. Like many New England boys, he had a strong desire for an education, and with limited means determined to have it if possible, including a college course. He studied Greek and Latin at Kimball Union Academy, in Meriden, New Hampshire. He was doomed to disappointment as to the college course, and when his preparation for it was well advanced he was led, much against his will, to abandon it, and to complete his academic studies at the New Hampton Institution, New Hampton, New Hampshire, then a popular Academy. His education was far more thorough and valuable because he was compelled to work for it, and that sturdy, self-reliant spirit, so manifest to all who knew him, was as much the result of his early orphaning as of inheritance.

A letter written late in life gives some light on those days. We quote from it: "Speaking of milking, it should be done rapidly and regularly, at about the same hour in the day, both morning and evening. Say so to ——. When I was fourteen I milked eight cows night and morning for a while, and did it well, working for six dollars a month and board in the summer, going to school and doing chores for my board in the winter, taking rank there as among the best. That way of life in the actual experience of it may seem hard and rough, but it pays. Those who started far ahead of me I left so far behind that they were out of sight years and years ago. The truth is that work pays, and it is only by work, mental or physical, or both, whereby any one attains to a real manhood."

Like many others who have had great influence on their generation, he went from the Academy directly to professional study. In Windsor, Vermont, he entered the law office of Aiken & Edgerton, a leading law firm in Windsor County, and was admitted to the bar in that county in June, 1841, at the age of twenty-four years. Soon after he opened an office in the town of Windsor, and met with such measure of professional success that he was enabled in a few years to pay off all the debts incurred in getting his education, and to assume the responsibilities of a family establishment. He is still remembered there as an eloquent public speaker, and he had the confidence of a large circle of clients.

He was married to Miss Lydia Wheelock Woodward, at the home of her brother, Henry M. Woodward, in Boston, April 27th, 1846. The cere-

mony was performed by Rev. George Punchard,
the well-known historian of Congregationalism.
She is a descendant of Myles Standish of early
Plymouth fame, and a great-granddaughter of
Rev. Eleazer Wheelock, D. D., the founder and
first President of Dartmouth College.

Though having a love for the profession of law,
and not in any sense an office seeker, political
honors were not wanting to him. He was frequently selected by the citizens of Windsor to fill
the offices of Town Agent and Justice of the
Peace. He thoroughly identified himself with the
interests of the place, and at one time was president of one of its most important manufacturing
establishments. In 1850, at the age of thirty-
three, he was elected from Windsor County to the
Senate of Vermont, and served the State in that
capacity through two successive sessions. He was
the youngest member of that body, unless Hon.
Homer E. Royce was his junior. His habits of
careful study, and his ability to see the bearing of
events on the future, were manifest here. Near the
close of the session in which he first served he
introduced a series of Union resolutions, which
passed both houses, and which were afterwards
widely published and much applauded.

The spirit of enterprise that possessed him
made the move to St. Louis in the new Southwest an easy one, and in 1857 we find him taking
up his abode in Missouri. Here was his residence
for many years, and it still continued his nominal
home and the center of his religious thought and
life when increasing feebleness made it imperative
that he should seek a milder climate in order to
prolong his days.

He entered heartily into the life of the growing
city, resuming the practice of law, and becoming
so well and favorably known that in 1864 he was
elected to the Lower House of the Missouri Legislature, and served the State as Chairman of the
important Committee on Ways and Means through
two successive sessions. It was the troublous period at the close of the war, and the duties of the
position were arduous and weighted with responsi-
bility, but were performed with general accept-
ance. His legal knowledge was so much appre-
ciated, and his acquaintance with the State and its
needs was so thorough, that when in 1865 the revision of the statute laws was undertaken, he was
chosen one of the committee of three for the purpose. Under the circumstances it was a difficult
task. The legislature took a recess from March

20th to November 1st of that year; it was intended that the revision should be accomplished in that time, which was all too short for the purpose. Quite a large number of the changes in the laws which were introduced into this work were the fruits of his experience and careful study. That they were timely is shown by the fact that much of his labor has remained, and still appears through the two revisions that have since been made. Of the one hundred and seventy-one chapters, he revised seventy-three himself, nearly one-half of the whole.

In 1868 he was elected to the Supreme Bench of the State, and served as one of the Judges of that high Court till January, 1872. He would undoubtedly have held the position longer. He said that the political changes which he foresaw would make a difference in the personnel of the Court at the end of his term, and he felt that he would be more comfortable elsewhere. So he resigned when he had yet two years to serve, and accepted the presidency of a prosperous manufacturing company, which at that time offered him pecuniary considerations and guarantees far more important than judicial honors.

In 1873 Judge Currier began to feel the approach of the enemy that pursued him remorselessly for nearly twenty years, and finally cost his life. He suffered from an attack of bronchitis, which proved intractable, and on the advice of his two physicians, Drs. J. B. Johnson and A. J. Steele, he spent the winter of 1873-4 in Florida. He was benefited by the climate, but not healed, and the bronchial troubles continued, so that he was compelled to give up St. Louis as a winter residence, and then to abandon it altogether, winding up his business, both professional and manufacturing, and devoting his time to matters in which he was especially interested.

It was during this winter in Florida that his oldest son, Edward, an unusually promising young man, sickened and died in St. Louis at his father's house. He was a graduate of Dartmouth College, standing high in his class, and when taken sick was the successful teacher of Natural Sciences in the St. Louis High School. Two letters written by the Judge from his retreat in Florida breathe the sweetest of Christian counsel, and show how thoroughly his own faith was grounded on the promises of God. From St. Augustine, under date of March 3rd, 1874, he writes: "My son, disease is upon us both. The time with us may be short. Let us cherish an unfaltering faith in our God, and in the reality of a life to come, where sickness and sorrow and dying are unknown. Let us aspire to that."

The religion of Judge Currier was of the practical, earnest type, and, strong man that he was, a word of comfort from him, or the use of a Scripture passage, had far more weight than it would from most men. We do not know at just what time his personal consecration to Christ began. He was an attendant on the services of the Old South Church in Windsor, contributing liberally to sustain it while residing there, and after his removal to St. Louis he furnished the Sunday School room, and donated to its library and to the general expenses of the Society. He united with the First Congregational Church in St. Louis, on confession of his faith, in April, 1858, one year after his arrival in the city. Rev. T. M. Post, D. .D., was its pastor, and among its members were strong men and women who were destined to exercise great influence on the religious life of the city and the whole Southwest.

At that time the First Church was located in what is now the eastern end of the city, and seemed far enough west for all time. But that

wonderful growth had begun which has made it
impossible to plant any churches in locations that
can be really permanent, and Christian people were
soon looking toward the setting sun in their plans
for the future. Rev. F. A. Armstrong had started a Sunday School in 1853, two miles back from
the river, and as he was called from the city immediately, others took up the work he had begun,
and carried it forward so earnestly and wisely that
Pilgrim Church was the result. Judge Currier became one of the toilers in the school, and had a
share in determining the policy that has brought
about glorious results. That policy was the concentration in one enterprise of a large portion of
the labor that was being put into many, and the
effort to make that one a power.

When in 1866 a lot was bought by Mr. Stephen
M. Edgell and Mr. James E. Kaime, and by them
presented "for the uses of an orthodox Congregational Church," Judge Currier was selected as one
of the building committee, and had a voice in all
the councils of the young organization. Pilgrim
Church was organized December 5th, 1866, and
Judge Currier acted as chairman of the meeting.
From the beginning he had great faith in the
future of the enterprise, and even after he had

ceased to be a resident of the city his membership remained there, his interest in everything pertaining to the church was unflagging, and much of his most generous giving continued to be done through its treasuries.

In later years he was always jealous for the early days of that church, and anxious that, in the wonderful growth that has come to it, the six years of the beginning should not be overlooked. A part of his own words may well be quoted here as referring to himself among others, though such was not his intent in using them; they are from his paper read at the twenty-fifth anniversary of the organization: "For four years Pilgrim Church had a hard road to travel. It was encompassed with enemies and rivals, and was bitterly assailed on every hand. Nevertheless it traveled on, and did its work as best it could. It took no step backward, nor did it turn to the right hand nor the left; but traveled straight on in faith and hope. It was a struggle for existence, but it never quailed. It never said die, and it had no intention of dying till results should be reached that would never die. This, I think, may be fairly called the heroic age of Pilgrim Church. Whoever speaks slightingly of it speaks unkindly or unadvisedly." This and much more he said in praise of the faith and constancy of those who were the Church of the early days, and he might truthfully have added "a large part of which I was." It expresses his own spirit exactly.

He was thoroughly grateful to any one who recognized these facts about the early times of the Church, and who intended to do them justice. To Rev. Simeon Gilbert, D. D., he wrote in 1886 as follows, the letter being inspired by an article by Dr. Gilbert: "What is unique in your eulogium (of Dr. Goodell) is the justice you do to the Church that stood behind him. The first six years of that Church remains to be written, and will probably always so remain. It nevertheless contains elements which a skillful dramatist might gather into a story full of interest and instruction."

One part of his own work in this noble Church he always contemplated with great satisfaction. Next to being a great leader, he has a right to rejoice who selects that leader. Next to being the most successful pastor and church builder of his generation, he who has a part in the choice of that pastor is worthy of honor. It is well known that all the consecration and ability that entered into

the organization of the Church would have failed
to realize its purpose without the right man at the
head. The coming of Dr. Goodell and his wife to
St. Louis at the time they did was an unusual instance of the workers and the hour perfectly fitted.
God had given them special preparation for the
task, and the young Church was ready to follow
where they led. Judge Currier was one of the
committee of two who went East commissioned to
find and recommend a pastor, and who dared to
believe that they could move the successful leader,
surrounded by a loving people and working under
the pleasantest circumstances imaginable, to an
unfinished hilltop in the then dirty and unattract-
ive city of St. Louis.

A quotation from the Judge's address at the
tenth anniversary of that pastorate gives the situation exactly: "The feeling was wide and deep in
Pilgrim Church, in the summer of 1872, that it
had reached a dangerously critical period in its
history. The conviction was strong that the whole
future of the Church was involved in the filling of
the then vacant pastorate. This conviction was
founded on facts and considerations of the most
substantial character. But I can not recount them
here. The conviction existed, and under its in-

fluence a search was made for a minister. The
search was long, thorough, patient, critical, and
was in the end rewarded by the acquisition of the
very best minister and the very best minister's
wife then to be found on the soil of America; at
least the best for the particular work here to be
done." Judge Currier was one of the two who
made that search, and his good judgment and that
of his companion on the committee was abundantly
proved by subsequent events.

On reaching the city with wife and children the
new pastor found a hearty welcome awaiting him
in the home of Judge Currier, and the three weeks
of sickness with which his ministry began were re-
lieved by the constant care and kind attentions of
this household. The story is best told by Mrs.
Goodell herself in the following letter to the
author: "Though many years have passed since
that cold November night, the night before
Thanksgiving, when my husband and I, with our
youngest child and maid, arrived in St. Louis from
the East, I shall never cease to remember with
gratitude the cordiality with which Judge Currier
and his dear wife welcomed us to their hospitable
home on Lucas avenue, nor the blazing fire that
had been kindled for us on the hearth of the

'Chamber of Peace' to which we were ushered after our wearisome ride that day from Chicago. Even then we were 'Pilgrims and Strangers' seeking a country; and if the truth were told we were sadly mindful of the blessed country from which we had come out. As we crossed the Father of Waters in the darkness of late evening our hearts were yearning for the shelter and companionship which this Christian home opened to us. In the few weeks that followed, these new friends had abundant occasion to show the genuineness of their welcome, for they were weeks of severe illness for my husband. The strain and heart-break of the farewells in the old home had proved too much for his sensitive and loving nature, and he was prostrated with fever on the very threshold of our new mission. Day after day he bore a severe burden, not for himself, but for the Church that had been anticipating the arrival of the new pastor, but were now unexpectedly called upon to wait after he was actually on the ground. In this trial of patience Judge Currier, strong and hopeful, did much to inspire the sick man with courage, and to lift anxiety from his mind by repeated assurances that no one would feel impatient at such a delay as this. The kindness of the

whole household was unceasing and Christlike in
spirit. The aid and encouragement which Judge
Currier gave at this particular time were characteristic of his subsequent life and history as a
leading and efficient member of the Church. He
was always alive to the great questions that concerned her welfare, and from a judicial, as well as
a Christian standpoint, he was able to bring a
weight of wisdom and counsel that was invaluable."

At the tenth anniversary of the settlement of
Dr. Goodell the principal address was delivered by
Judge Currier, who was at that time able to be
present and take the part assigned him. It was in
his best vein, full of his old-time faith in the
enterprise and joy in its success. At the twenty-
fifth anniversary of the organization of the
Church, observed in December, 1891, a paper contributed by him was read, reviewing the early days
of the Church, and showing the value of its beginning. Quotations from both these addresses
have already been given. His part in these anniversary occasions shows how keenly his interest in
the' affairs of the city, and especially its religious
life, remained to the end with him. He was an
exile from home, trying to prolong life as long as
God should will, and suffering constantly while in

the body, but intent on doing his work so long as his life should be spared.

For eighteen or nineteen years he battled with disease, and fled from one clime to another to escape the extremes of heat and cold that aggravated his malady. His trip to Florida in 1873–4, his subsequent stay for a season in California, and his semi-annual migrations with the birds, were all in search of health, or at least of such comfort as it might be possible to find with the hand of disease resting constantly upon him. His winters were spent for several years in Georgia, at Marietta and Thomasville, and his summers in Colorado, mostly at Greeley. And in all these places he kept his hold upon the matters vital to the religious life of the denomination to which he belonged, and was in constant touch with it.

He felt great satisfaction in having battled so long and successfully against death; he had no fear of it; he spoke laughingly one day of the fact that the doctors had practically given him up years before, and said, "I have baffled the doctors for nearly fifteen years. They told me I could not get well; I shall go some time; I am ready when God calls me, but I feel a sort of satisfaction in having lived these years." The work of these years will be spoken of later in this volume, as it related chiefly to other churches than the one in which he was a member.

The end came at last, as it does to the strongest, and at Lithia Springs, Georgia, he passed away peacefully July 25th, 1892. All arrangements for the inevitable had been carefully made years before, and the body was taken to St. Louis, where, in the Church he loved, and to the starting of which he had given the best years of his life, the funeral services were held. His pastor, Dr. Stimson, was too far away to be called back, and the service was conducted by one who had known him long and intimately, and had cause to feel grateful for his interest in every organization started in the name of the Master. The hymns sung were: "Lead, Kindly Light," "Rock of Ages," and "Sleep Thy Last Sleep, Free From Care and Sorrow." The service was simple and brief, as would have been his wish, and the weary, worn-out body was laid to rest in the beautiful Bellefontaine Cemetery.

CHAPTER II.

TRAITS OF CHARACTER.

" Sooner or later that which is now life shall be poetry, and every fair and manly trait shall add a richer strain to the song."

—Emerson.

CHAPTER II.

TRAITS OF CHARACTER.

True character is never the result of chance. One distances another in the race of life because he has qualities that fit him to take the lead. Some men are certain to win the respect of others and become makers of events, because they have carefully prepared themselves for the crises that demand them. This chapter will be devoted to a brief mention of the most notable traits of character in Judge Currier as recognized by his acquaintances, those that entitled him to the name of a Christian Lawyer. If the lawyer is not made so emphatic as the Christian, it is because everybody sees the lawyer, while the Christian is known to those whose lives and work are especially influenced by him. This is not intended to be a claim that Christian lawyers are uncommon; pastors of churches are aware of the sterling qualities of the large number of men in the legal profession who are quietly and unobtrusively serving their Master in daily life, and whose influence upon the churches is of the greatest value. Rather let this life be taken as a type, of which there are many in the land, and their tribe is continually on the increase. A friend wrote to his son: "Your father was a wonderful man. I have not seen another at all like him. And he has left his impress on his age in a way that can never be effaced." It is impossible to put all of any life upon paper, and this sketch must necessarily be imperfect and unsatisfactory, but we aim to speak of some of those traits that will make any life noticeable.

His thoroughness was remarked by all who knew him. It was either born in him or developed by the circumstances of his early life. At any rate, it appeared to his schoolmates, and is recalled by some of them now after the lapse of threescore years. An old-time friend in Windsor, Vermont, writes concerning him: "I can hardly say we were life-long friends, though that was very nearly the case; our acquaintance commenced at the old brick school house on the Common in this village —I think the winter that I was about twelve, and he some four or five years older. I remember that at the time he set an example to us younger ones of studiousness, which if we had followed more closely would have been to our advantage. From that time on I can not remember when he was not a great student, and I rejoice at the grand success in life which he made: evidently he started with just that determination, and he accomplished his undertaking." Take notice that what was true of him at school was as true all his life.

To one who looked to him for counsel he wrote: "Pray be a little more accurate in your statements. When I was of your age (24) I was called the 'gentleman of critical accuracy,' and a long life has shown me that accuracy is one element of character of the highest importance. This is my twentieth page, and I have indulged in no romance, or intended to write a superfluous sentence, line, or a word."

He was one of the best business men. A paragraph in one of his letters is thoroughly characteristic: "Mr. ——— writes you on *Love*, and does it well, but I write you on business. Love in a cabin is good and to be cherished, but it may come to grief unless the business prospers. I believe in love; I believe also in a gorgeous sunset and the dreams of poets. These are real, real as business and more lasting than the dollars of commerce; but they are not everything, not every-

thing here on earth, however they may be beyond the river. There is a time for all things,
and this is the very time to close this letter."
His habits of thoroughness, promptness, and conservatism were helpful to him in all business trans-
actions. He was very shrewd, and enjoyed a good
trade more than most men. He had a habit of
going through any matter he had under consideration, and making himself fully master of it. He
was a man of powerful intellect, though simple
and clear in his style. His reading was very ex-
tensive; he read and enjoyed such authors as
Schlegel, Darwin, Spencer, Lecky and Froude. He
read the Bible as he would a history, referring to
maps and authorities, and studied for hours what
he had read. He was not what we usually understand by a Bible student, but he read and studied
the different books repeatedly, searching them
critically, and forming opinions of his own concerning them.

A natural result of this was that he had firm
convictions on every subject. A friend says:
" Nothing he undertook was ever slighted." The
secretaries of our benevolent societies remember
well how long and forcefully he persisted in his
correspondence with them, never letting up once

when he had undertaken to accomplish a purpose,
until he received assurances that were satisfactory
to himself. In a letter written in 1880 he said:
"It is not spasms of enthusiasm and war cries that
promise success in the sheep business, or any business, but thoughtful persistence in well doing day
by day and every day the year round." This
entered into all his business life; he demanded
the same thoroughness from all who came under
his influence. No individual or church could get
aid from him until all the conditions he made were
fulfilled to the letter; everything must be in black
and white; he would take nothing for granted;
and those conditions were sometimes heavy, but
always for the good of the one who had to meet
them. It is no wonder he was successful in all
he undertook; one who enjoys a good trade, is
strictly honest, exact in all his dealings, giving his
attention to details and demanding of all under
him the most careful accounting, must succeed;
and it is true of Judge Currier that as a business
man, whether in law or trade, he was a success.
This habit of thoroughness he carried to the last.
As the end drew near he was asked if he had any
message to send, any word to leave, any instruc-
tions to give while there was yet time, and he re-

sponded: "No; everything is arranged." Everything had been arranged for years, so that the family should have the least amount of care and annoyance, and so that all his purposes might be carried out according to his wishes.

This habit of thoroughness was of great value to the Church in which the greater part of his Christian life was spent. There is no period in a church's history so critical, none needing such patient care, as its first few years. There is no place where thoroughness counts for so much as time passes as in the shaping of affairs legal and in the Manual at the start. All the beginnings of Pilgrim Church were well planned. The Manual was carefully framed; the legal matters relating to it were fully attended to; Judge Currier was one of those most prominent in these affairs, and his characteristic thoroughness marked all that was done.

Nothing delighted him more than to learn of the development of this habit in churches; slipshod ways of doing the Master's work were detestable to him. In replying to a friend who wrote of an effort to enlist the interest and co-operation of all the members of a distant church, he says: "The church seems to have awakened to a new and better and more enterprising life. That calling out of the entire membership at the annual meeting was a fine thought apparently well executed. It shows the church alive and in action." Surrounded as he was much of his life by many who were not noted for care about the future, it is impossible to measure the value of his influence, especially on the new churches he helped to form.

A man who is thorough is pretty sure to be prompt. This was eminently true of the Judge. The letters he preserved show that he answered many of them the day they were received; all of them were replied to within a week, unless sickness prevented. Friends were sometimes astonished at getting a reply almost before return mail, to propositions involving the expenditure of large sums of money. His mind acted quickly, his judgment as to the subject involved was already formed, and he wanted to see immediate results. " Don't let the grass grow under your feet," was a favorite expression of his in relation to the work to be done. This habit grew upon him in later life, as if the uncertainty resulting from his weak condition made him doubly anxious to see things secure while he was able to attend to them himself. The King's business required haste.

These statements relate entirely to matters
which many put aside or leave to be administered
by others as they grow weak and draw near the
end. When he gave counsel he longed to see the
resulting good. When he made a pledge of money
he was eager to pay it, and chafed at delay. He
was not satisfied if a church in a good location
was not properly housed, and when he knew the
facts he was prompt to write an urgent request for
immediate action.

The qualities that made him a good lawyer and
a just judge were of the greatest service to the
cause of Christ. His excellent judgment was remarked by all who had dealings with him. His
habits of thoroughness and promptness were a
combination that enabled him to see all the bearings of a subject at a glance. His mind was never
made up from impulse, nor from a desire to be on
the popular side. "He was accustomed to carefully weigh the facts bearing upon any subject,
and his opinions were formed after careful consideration, and were generally sound and safe to follow." So writes one who knew him intimately
for many years. We give here a sentence from
another letter which has been used in a former
chapter: "He was far-sighted in judgment, and

did not let minor obstacles stand in the way of the onward movement of affairs." A leading business man says of him: "We know he was a man of strong opinions, and that when he had made up his mind he maintained his conviction; but his views were generally so well taken that they were readily accepted, and no mistake made in following his lead."

The same peculiarity had been noticed when he was on the bench; it takes good judgment to be brief and clear; it was said of his decisions that it was impossible to misunderstand them; they were easy to see through. He was satisfied with rendering a brief and concise opinion, rather than a long and showy one. This quality, valuable alike in law and gospel practice, is so well expressed in the notice of his death in the *Rocky Mountain Congregationalist* that we quote it here: "He was a good adviser. He saw always the things to be done. He could brook no shams, and would countenance no subterfuges. If sometimes he seemed imperious it was because he saw clearly, felt deeply, and could never be a policy man. He was a hard man for an insincere man to meet. True men found he had the gentlest of natures and the warmest of hearts. He had convictions in theol-

ogy, in church polity, and in the practical working
of our missionary enterprises at home and abroad.
He was a statesman in his wisdom."

This good judgment went in later years into all
the great concerns of the denomination he loved.
He was a Congregationalist from principle, and believed that the polity and doctrine are essential to
the good of American Christianity. He was impatient at the tardiness of others in seeing the opportunities that are before us. He read the signs
of the times as they apply to the Master's kingdom, and he felt that unless we adapt our work to
the changing conditions of life and thought we
may lose a chance that can never be had again. It
is a significant fact that nearly all the principles
for which he contended in the management of our
church and missionary operations are generally
accepted by the denomination now, and some of
them at least have to do with the renewed and enlarged growth that is coming to us, and the assur-
ance that the belief and polity of the Pilgrims are
not to be behind in molding the future of our
loved country. He saw twenty-five years ahead of
his day, and did his best to make others see as he
did.

Coupled with these qualities was a high sense of

honor; no one ever found in him the slightest
shading from what was strictly honest. All his
dealings were such as would bear the closest scru-
tiny. Many men are, or think themselves, religious, but seem to forget that sterling integrity is a
large part of Christian life. Some are strictly honest, who do not know that their impulse toward
honesty comes from God, and they neglect to give
Him the glory. But in this man the highest and
noblest faith was united with the greatest care in
the most trifling affairs. This made him an uncom-
fortable man to deal with if one was not careful
to render strict justice. He was unwilling that any
one should be dealt with unfairly, and a suspicion
on his part that another had received scant justice
was enough to set him to writing letters to have
the wrong made right. One of these letters to a
friend contains a long and vigorous statement of
the fine qualities of another person, and the nobil-
ity of that life, because he felt that in a tribute
rendered only a part of the truth had been told.

In another letter to the same party he speaks of
receiving a copy of the report of the New England
dinner of that year, and discusses the addresses
made there. Among other things he speaks of an
allusion made to General Lyon: " The most im-

pressive thing in ————'s speech is his quotation
from Webster's Bunker Hill oration, applying the
sentiment to Lyon, and as I think with perfect
justice and appropriateness.   Lyon was a remarkable man.   His career was short, but it was
brilliant, and displayed wonderful energy and mili-
tary skill.   No other General accomplished so much
in so short a time—or anything like it—during the
first year of the war.   He saved Missouri."   Then
follows in strong language an expression of his
disgust that Lyon was hampered by the negligence
or incompetence of others, and finally led to his
death when he could not be spared.   He felt that
in the strong records that were made by other officers before the close of the war we should not
forget the services of one of the few men who,
when the war began, saw that it meant energetic
action and hard fighting to the end.

This fine sense of honor made it certain that no
one would ever question his Christianity.   There
are some classes of men who from their employment are more liable than others to suspicion as
Christians, and the slightest flaw in their lives
brings disgrace on the Christianity they profess.
Twenty years ago in an eastern city a lawyer was
elected to the office of deacon in an important

church; he rose promptly, and speaking with deep feeling, thanked the church for their confidence in him, but declined the office, giving as his reason the fact that so many people regard " lawyer" and " liar" as synonymous terms. A leading member stated immediately that the church were proud of the fact that they had a member whose daily life was a flat contradiction of that impression. The lawyer was again elected, and though he has since occupied many high positions, and political honors have been showered upon him, not a blot has ever been found on his character. No one can estimate the value of such lives. It is impossible to learn here how many are stimulated to a better life, or saved from a worse one, by the constant example of men whose professional life is spotless. Such was that of Judge Currier. However others were led to differ with him they were compelled to admit that he followed his convictions, and never violated his own conscience.

He was a man of frank, almost brusque manner, and sometimes severe in speech; and those who knew him but slightly might get the impression that he was not kindly; but no man had a kinder heart. A former St. Louis pastor writes: " Judge Currier's friendship and fellowship were most de-

lightful to me.   He was a blessing and help to me
during all my St. Louis pastorate, and I shall ever
cherish his memory with gratitude." He delighted
in helping in any way those needing his assistance.
No friend who came to him in trouble of any kind
was ever turned away without sympathy and sound
advice, and often when circumstances required it,
and he was able, more substantial aid was rendered.   He delighted in lifting burdens from
others.   His accounts show a large number of
cases where he paid the expenses of men in their
attendance on important meetings. In one instance
he thought the exchange of two pastors for a
Sunday would bring the two churches nearer together, and he paid the expense of the exchange,
amounting to nearly fifty dollars.   In a large number of letters he left, received from others, no expression is so common as that of thanks.   His life
in later years was a continual reception of letters
of gratitude from those he had in various ways
benefited.   One on which he made a note signify-
ing the end of a long transaction, is a letter of
thanks for favors extending over many years.

This spirit of love and helpfulness was manifest
nowhere more plainly than in relation to his own
family, especially in times of distress.   His letters

to his son Edward, a little while before the latter's death, give him directions for the supply of everything that in any way can relieve pain or give comfort while life lasts, and express a tenderness of feeling unusual in one of such strong character, and who rarely showed feeling in the presence of others. A relative, after his death, wrote as follows: "He was a good, great man; he was a maker of events. He left his impress upon the world as he came in contact with it. In a marked sense this was true of his family and connections. He was a helper to all his father's family. It almost seemed as though he had a God-given mission to his father's family."

He had a deep interest in young men. The young people who came to Pilgrim Church in the early days had cause to remember with pleasure his kindness to them, and his efforts to make them feel at home, especially if they were strangers in the city. His house was open to them, and the same hearty welcome that awaited the new pastor and his family was extended to all who would be comforted by it. This interest grew in many cases into tenderness in time of need, and helpfulness when burdens were heavy. But as his life drew toward its close his heart went out especially toward his grandchildren. His letters to them show an appreciation of their thoughtfulness in little things, and a joy in whatever interested them that is hardly to be expected in an old man. They loved to remember his birthday, and send him some little token of affection, and it always drew from him a grateful letter and expressions of renewed joy in their love for him.

One who had had opportunity to see the warm side of his nature, and was on terms of intimacy with him, wrote on receipt of the news of his death: "So ends a long and well spent life. It is a great blessing to have had such a father. His clear and vigorous intellect, the breadth of mental vision which manifestly widened as he advanced in years, a thing as fine as it is rare to see, his strong and positive spirit, his deep, earnest and practical religious convictions, made him altogether a remarkable and valuable man. I shall always remember the friendship with which he honored me with pleasure." Another, whose intimate acquaintance with him was in the earlier days of his residence in St. Louis, says: "While a great stickler for what he considered right, he was genial, whole-souled, and an earnest, sincere, upright, Christian gentleman."

He was an optimist. Very few have large and lasting influence who are not. He saw the bright side of God's dealings with men and nations. When others were hopeless he was studying events, and saw a brighter future. To a friend, younger than himself, who had expressed some fears about the future of a great enterprise, he wrote half playfully: "I think you a little too pessimistic for a youngster on the sunny side of fifty." He saw the brilliant future of his denomination, and even when good men differed with him on points which he considered vital as to the policy to be pursued, he never doubted that all would be well. So of Pilgrim Church; when it was a struggling infant he was certain that it was born for a great purpose, and that its future was assured. While many were magnifying the dangers, he was making the most of the present, and was certain that better times were coming. This habit did not fail when his own life was in danger. He weighed probabilities as to his living longer as calmly as he would any business matter. He was thankful for any cessation of pain or inconvenience, and always ready to give God the praise for his relief. Two years before his death he wrote at the close of a letter on a special matter of business: "I feel grateful to God every day for His goodness and the bounty of His providence, and for the hopes of the future."

He was strict in his ideas of the value of Christian institutions; all that represented principle was precious, and he viewed with anything but complacency the tendency to the worldly use of the Christian Sabbath. His early training was among the careful observers of God's day, and with his habit of forecasting the future he saw the inevitable result of loose ideas concerning it. With his children he was strict, and demanded proper observance of all these things. He took exception to a sermon delivered in Pilgrim Church in the early days, because he thought it advocated a tendency toward Sabbath breaking. Yet, with all this he was not behind the times; he adapted himself to the changing civilization in the midst of which he lived, and believed heartily in all real progress. He was a good balance wheel to keep others from going too far in the direction of seeming liberality.

Underlying all these traits, and largely responsible for them, was a firm faith in the Law and the Gospel as revealed from God. His belief was not merely a creed, though he had a creed well thought out, and it had much to do with his life. With him religion was a practical thing, a vital relation to his Heavenly Father, such a relation that he founded all his thought and action upon it. He had no doubts about the promises, and was confident that the Providence that had created and sustained him was equal to all his needs for this life and the next. This faith lent a vigor and beauty not often seen to his later years of suffering and weakness. He viewed without fear or regret the decay of the body and the approach of certain death. There was nothing for him to fear, and he had no misgivings. The Savior who had been with him all the years was with him to the end. A month before that end came he wrote: "My strength does not come, so I must limit myself in writing. I have fallen in weight to one hundred and forty pounds, and so far as I can judge am still on the down grade. You will see that I have but little physical stamina to go on. This world is to some extent losing its attractions for me. My thoughts are turning more to the inward and the invisible, and less to the outward, even in ecclesiastical affairs. Where shall I find Him, O! My Soul, who yet is everywhere? Not in circling heights, or depths, but in the conscious breast."

To his grandchildren he wrote four months be-

fore he died as cheerfully and pleasantly as if he
felt no pain, and sent a special message to every
one, replying to their letters and mementos sent on
his seventy-fifth birth-day.   The letter begins as
follows : " Dear Children, I thank you very much
for your remembrance of me this day.   This ' old
house ' still stands, but whether it can be propped
up another year is quite uncertain.   It is very old
and very much out of repair. ' Nature and reason
tell us all this shattered frame ere long must
fall.' "   The quotations are from a poem written in
her eighty-seventh year by the wife of one of
the founders of Oberlin College to a lady in her
ninety-ninth year.   Judge Currier was attracted by
it, and felt that it expressed his own condition.
The stanza quoted is as follows :

> " Nature and reason tell us all
>   This shattered frame ere long must fall.
>   When, how, and where, unknown.
>   We'll leave that to the Architect,
>   And trust His wisdom to direct
>   The taking of it down."

His character is well summed up in a letter from
one who knew him as only two or three others
did : " He was no saint; he was simply a grand,
strong, affectionate, successful man, whose methods in business matters were so woven into his na-

ture, that when his strength had almost entirely left him his trembling fingers were forced by his masterful will to grasp a pen, and by one last scrawling signature to complete the benefaction of a lifetime. He closed the transaction by his own act, and this closing act was more potent through his weakness than the strong, virile generosity of the previous forty years."

CHAPTER III.

HIS INFLUENCE ON THE CHURCH.

———

" Life is a mission. Every other definition of life is false, and leads all who accept it astray. Religion. science. philosophy. though still at variance upon many points. all agree in this, that every existence is an aim."

—*Mazzini.*

CHAPTER III.

A mind like Judge Currier's, capable of grasping the largest and the most complicated subjects, naturally shows its power in the life and work of his denomination. He was a shaper of events, and has left his impress on church life at large. There is no department of church administration that has not felt his touch. His correspondence contains the handwriting of nearly every secretary of a Congregational benevolent society who lived in his time, and some of those secretaries consumed weeks in answering his questions, meeting his conditions, or discussing with him the proper policy to be pursued in their work. His interest descended also to the most minute affairs, and men in every part of the country who were struggling with hopeful, but financially weak, enterprises had reason to bless him. The editors of a small religious paper express their gratitude for a timely and large check; the writer of a pamphlet does the same for

help in paying the expense of its publication. The
President of Colorado College is rejoiced at his
founding a $1000 scholarship. He several times
helped Drury College in its hours of distress.
These are samples of many acts of the same sort,
done so quietly that none but the recipients knew
of them.

He was full of denominational loyalty, and it
did not make him one whit less a Christian; he
loved his Church as he loved his home, and he
loved every other church in consequence. He rejoiced in all real progress in other denominations;
but he toiled for the upbuilding of one, because he
believed in the principles it represents. His voice
and pen had a large influence in bringing about the
gradual change of policy that has come, and the
clippings from the press which he saved showed
that this topic was one uppermost in his mind.
With him a polity worth having was worth perpetuating, and he deemed it supreme folly to leave
its future to those inimical to it or to chance, or
even to Providence. He believed that an energetic,
aggressive policy would win victories for the whole
Kingdom of Christ, and that the Congregational
method was the best one to employ for the purpose.

Under these circumstances it was quite natural that he should be more interested in the Home Missionary Society than in any other benevolent organization, because that is the medium through which churches can be planted and nourished. In filling out the schedule for systematic beneficence in his own church he massed his giving largely on that society, because he felt that just then its methods of collection were not so thorough as they should be. He advocated the adoption of the energetic collection methods of the American Board. He was anxious that the annual meetings should be taken out of the State of New York, that it might be brought in touch with the life of the churches all over the country.

He was not always in accord with the leaders of these missionary bodies, and did not hesitate to express his dissent. He took issue with one of the secretaries of the American Board of Commissioners for Foreign Missions, because in an article in the *Congregationalist* he advocated giving for foreign work as much as for all the societies whose field lies in the United States. It was no spirit of opposition to foreign missions that led him to take such ground, but a sense of the overwhelming importance of converting America to Christ,

and the belief that on this depends the existence of
every benevolent society we have. As one outside
all these organizations he had a different idea of
the proportion of things from those who were toil-
ing to further the interests of one. This frequently brought him into seeming antagonism with
some of them, and led to long and spicy correspondence.

Long before the fact was generally acknowl-
edged, he held that there was a great work for
Congregationalists among the white people of the
South. He thought it a narrow and bad policy to
expend all our force on one race, even though it
were down-trodden. He was always friendly to the
society that makes its chief effort for the conver-
sion and education of the blacks; and one of his
firmest friends is now and has been for many years
a secretary of that society. But he saw that by
spending all our strength in the South in this one
line we were throwing away a golden opportunity
for reaching a class that need what we have to
give, and are likely to be greatly influenced by us
through coming years. In an interview with the
editor of a paper, at a time when this subject was
much under discussion, he said: "Congregationalists should go South for the same reason that they

should go West, or go anywhere else. There is a large and hopeful field there for Congregational activities, particularly in business centers where northern people gather, such as Atlanta, Ga., and Jacksonville, Fla. In the near future in its business thrift, and opinions of its controlling population in its whole civilization, Florida promises to be a northern State." These words were uttered at a time when thousands did not believe them to be true. They represent a dead issue now and are only quoted as showing how well he foresaw a future to which the eyes of many were closed.

In the same large spirit he believed that the denomination he loved should not be limited by any boundaries that do not limit the whole Christian religion. There was a time when Congregationalism was supposed by many of its children to belong only to New England. It spread beyond the Hudson, and then they talked about a "New England Zone," and limited their efforts to the "lost sheep of the house of New England." In process of time the work of consecrated men in several quarters, notably in Missouri, proved that the limitation of our polity in any way is unwise, and led to a revision of the policy of several of our benevolent organizations. At just this time Judge

Currier was asked what was most needed to develop the denomination and cause real growth, and he replied: "Organization, unity, and denominational purpose. Congregationalism has been provincial. If it is to live and flourish it must be national."

At the time when some northern papers were publishing attacks on the American Home Missionary Society for its determination to go into the South wherever there were proper openings, the Judge replied to one of these articles, and gave expression to his views and feelings as follows: "Your correspondent, who is so unfriendly to this progressive movement, signs himself 'A Consistent Congregationalist,' and so he is; that is, he is consistent with the ancient New England tradition that a Congregational Church was not to be trusted out at night after dark, and that the spread of such churches beyond the confines of happy New England was not to be encouraged." Again he wrote to the *Advance* in 1865: "It has been said that Congregationalism as a system of ecclesiastical order and government is organized on principles far out toward the millennium. Can this delicate thing, this millennial plant, abide the civilization of the South? Can it germinate and grow there? Has it any business down there anyway? Will the southern people tolerate an ecclesiastical government of the people, for the people, and by the people? These questions and others like them have been asked many times over, and have generally been answered in the negative. Congregationalism could go to India and Japan, to Turkey and China, but the fearful and the unbelieving have protested that it had no mission among white people in the southern half of our country. Still, notwithstanding these protests, Congregationalism has actually gone South, and gone there to stay and grow up with the country."

He was strong in his conviction that we need to exercise greater care over weak churches. In a time when every effort to emphasize fellowship, as well as autonomy, among Congregationalists was opposed bitterly, he was not afraid to speak of them as a "denomination," and to advocate strongly and persistently a more thorough form of organization, and a more practical sympathy with struggling churches. In a letter to the *Advance* written in 1883 from Florida, he gives utterance to his feeling of annoyance that our church in Jacksonville was suffering for lack of active fellowship and proper oversight, while the Methodist

Church in the same place was taking a leading position because of the organization of Methodism for the purpose of caring for such points. He was delighted when his letter brought out the fact that the Home Missionary Society had already made preparations to do the thing he advocated, and was commissioning men for several points in the South, among them the one about which he wrote. He was unwilling that a church anywhere should wither and die because it was left in its weakness to care for itself.

There is one interesting matter of Congregational Church history that ought to be known to all. That is the genesis of the National Council. There are times when a subject is in the air; things are ripe, and only the right start is needed for a forward movement. It must be a determined man, of firm convictions and good judgment, who gives the impulse. Judge Currier always believed that as a denomination we erred in not making our organization more compact, and developing a more ardent love for our principles. No man was more jealous than he for the preservation of those principles, and he feared lest the knowledge of them be lost through carelessness and indifference. He saw with shame the rapid strides made by other denominations, who had, as he thought, less admirable purposes and possibilities. He felt that the principles that led men to brave the dangers of sea and land, and face the perils of savage men and more savage disease, were worth perpetuating, and that as the country grows in importance and population it becomes necessary to adapt our methods to the changed conditions and centralize our thought.

He believed we ought to be something besides a raft of logs, liable at any moment to fall to pieces. He expressed his sentiments freely in conversation and in the press, and found others who believed like himself. In April, 1864, as he went up the river by steamer to attend at Beardstown a meeting of the Southern Association of Illinois, with which the First Church in St. Louis was then connected, he explained his views to Dr. T. M. Post, his pastor, and found him in hearty accord with himself. The matter was discussed then and at the meeting, which was held April 14–17, 1864, and the result was the adoption of the following resolution :

"WHEREAS, in the past history of our country the existence of slavery in all the Southern and Southwestern States of the American Union has been an insuperable obstacle to the successful prosecution of the home missionary enterprise in these States; and

"WHEREAS, God in his providence is removing that system of iniquity from the land, and opening these vast and fertile regions to the free propagation of the Gospel and the founding of churches according to the form planted on this continent by the Pilgrim Fathers; therefore,

"*Resolved,* That this Association request the General Association of Illinois, at its approaching meeting at Quincy, to take into consideration the expediency of inviting a convention of American Congregationalists to assemble in September or October next, to consider the relation of the Congregational churches of the United States to this vast and unlooked-for enlargement of the field of our great home missionary enterprise, and to adopt such measures in relation to it as shall seem best suited to the exigencies of the solemn crisis to which we are brought."

Years after, in writing upon this subject, Judge Currier says: "Our National Council was developed from this point. The originators of the movement had in view from the start the results now reached, namely, the establishment of a

body, national in character, which should hold
stated meetings at fixed intervals for the consideration of subjects of common interest to all the
churches, having special reference to the benevolent, educational and missionary work devolved
upon them." The originators to whom he refers
were Judge Currier himself, and such men as Dr.
T. M. Post, Dr. J. M. Sturtevant, and others of
the band of men of rare gifts and great consecration who were then laying foundations of national
importance in the Mississippi Valley.

The General Association of Illinois, at its meeting in May, 1867, appointed a committee on "The
Results of the National Congregational Council,
held in Boston, June, 1865." In its report,
printed in full in an appendix to the published
minutes of Illinois for that year, this committee
says: "The call for the Boston Council originated in this State. It was suggested early in the
spring of 1864 by Warren Currier, Esq., of St.
Louis, a delegate from the Congregational Church
in that city to the Southern Association of Illinois.
The Triennial Convention at Chicago responded in
April of that year, and at Quincy, May 27th following, this General Association of Illinois 'Resolved, That a convention be invited,' etc.,

and all the other State associations in the country, New Hampshire only excepted, concurred in the call." One who was present at the Triennial Convention says: "When Dr. Post brought to the Triennial Convention of the Chicago Seminary this idea of a National Council, it seemed to have been an inspired proposition."

In a letter to the *Congregationalist* in the issue of August 6th, 1874, Dr. J. E. Roy makes use of the completion of the Eads' Bridge across the Mississippi as follows: "Judge Warren Currier, who is now going east from St. Louis via Chicago, reports his crossing the river upon that bridge of arches. The traveling public will be glad to know that that break-neck ferry is no longer to be one of the startling risks of those who visit that great city. As the time is now coming for the session of the established National Council, it will be well to remember that that idea, now so happily incorporated into our Church system, can be traced back through the meetings at Oberlin and Boston and Chicago, and through the Southern Association of Illinois, to the brain of one of its members, the worthy Judge named above; and so the bridge of Congregational fellowship has been made to span the river of indifference."

The man who had first put in workable form the idea, then new and untried, of a Congregational Council that should be more far-reaching than its own session, was of course present, and a participator in its work. He was one of the three delegates from Missouri, the other two being Dr. T. M. Post, of St. Louis, and Rev. J. M. Sturtevant, Jr., then pastor at Hannibal. The Judge was a member of the committee to nominate permanent officers. He was made chairman of the important Committee on Home Evangelization. The report of that committee, in which his hand is easily discerned, is a masterly presentation of the needs of the country at that time, and in it is sounded the cry reiterated by him again and again for aggressive, intelligent pushing of our polity among all classes at the South. The report received words of strong commendation from the special committee appointed to consider it, and had much to do with shaping opinion for the energetic campaign in Missouri that was then beginning, and has given what strength Congregationalism has there now. One who was himself active in that Council says: "His giving birth to the idea of the Boston Council, and his serving as chairman of its committee on Home Evangelization, took him up to high tide in his repute as a wide and enthusiastic worker for the cause of the Master as represented by the Congregational churches.''

He was not content with having originated a council different in scope from those which had preceded it, but watched carefully for the opportunity to carry out his original purpose and make it a regular part of the Congregational polity. Public opinion on the subject was forming in the right direction, and in many quarters his idea was discussed and favored by others. In 1870, April 27th, Rev. R. B. Thurston, of Stamford, Conn., introduced into the Pilgrim Memorial Convention, at Chicago, a resolution favoring the scheme of a permanent national organization. This resolution was referred to the business committee, which decided pretty promptly not to report it. At this stage Judge Currier arrived in the convention. Learning what had been done in the committee, he sought out one of its members with whom he was personally acquainted and explained to him his view of the matter and his idea of the importance of it to the denomination. At Judge Currier's earnest solicitation the committee reconsidered its action, and finally agreed on and reported a resolution recommending the institution of a "perma-

nent annual or triennial conference." This resolution was adopted by the convention. A little
later Judge Currier wrote to Dr. W. W. Patton,
then editor of the *Advance*, an earnest letter on
the subject. Dr. Patton made a part of that letter
the text for a stirring editorial in the *Advance* of
June 9th, 1870. One month later, in the *Congregational Quarterly* for July, 1870, appeared an
able article from the pen of Rev. R. B. Thurston,
the author of the resolution mentioned above.
This article was entitled "A National Conference."
These communications, the letter of Judge Currier, the editorial of Dr. Patton called forth by it,
and the article by Dr. Thurston, revived the
scheme, and the Oberlin Council was the outcome.

The fact is that the time had come when the
National Council was a necessity; leading men
east and west were thinking about it. Many were
fearful of centralization of power and interference
with the autonomy of the churches. A few men,
of whom Judge Currier was the leader, were full
of an opposite fear, that the denomination they
loved would fail of its mission for lack of unity of
purpose. Their words, spoken and written,
brought about the desired result, and the wisdom
of the movement is proved by the outcome. Per-

haps it would be claiming too much to say that
any one man was responsible for the whole forward march, but no one man did so much effective
work toward it as did Judge Currier. The Boston
Council was his own suggestion. The Oberlin
Council naturally followed, and yet but for him it
would have been several years delayed.

He watched with deep solicitude the growth and
character of the Council, and often wrote upon it
in private correspondence and in the press, urging
those who had influence in the meetings to shape
them for practical results. His thought is well
expressed in an article in the *Advance* already
quoted, where he says: " Precisely what American Christianity most needs to-day, next to the
baptism of the Spirit, is in my judgment the rais-
ing up of an array of ecclesiastical politicians in
all the denominations—men of might, whose devotion to the general cause shall consume and burn
out petty rivalries; statesmen who shall apply the
rules of prudence, economy and common sense to
the management of church and denominational affairs, subordinating that which is less to that
which is more important." This is exactly what
the judge was trying to bring about during all
those weary years when he was fighting death, and

his influence was great in leading others to mingle practical sense with consecration.

His idea of the Council was that it should be in every way a working body. Some were afraid that it would be prying into what did not concern it, or interfering with the prerogatives of others. He thought that every other body we have should be in some sense subordinate to it, especially that all our benevolent societies should pass in review before it as the highest representative body we have; not merely for the purpose of asking aid, but for careful examination of their methods in the interest of economy and better administration. It is quite possible that if his thought had been fully carried out we might have been spared some of the trying experiences of the last few years. He hoped that a consolidation of some of these societies might result eventually, without impairing their efficiency or lessening the amount given, but with greater economy in handling funds and better work in the field. He sent communications to each Provisional Committee of a Council, making suggestions about live topics, fearful always lest it should degenerate into a mere expression of good will, doing nothing and influencing nobody. If some brethren found him constantly appealing to them it was because he realized the dangers, and felt that one serious blunder might imperil the existence of that to which he had given much of his best thought. His views are well summed up in an article of his in the *Congregationalist* for September 16th, 1886:

" Beyond question the Council is in its structure and aim denominational. It represents Congregational churches exclusively, and is as exclusively denominational as is the Baptist General Convention, or the Presbyterian General Assembly. It is not distinguishable from the latter as not being denominational, but as being, like the Baptist General Convention, without legislative or judicial powers. It is in no sense an ecclesiastical court. It tries no cases and makes no laws. Its aims are wholly different. * * * It has been said that the Council is an experiment. It is so. It came near going by the board three years ago; would in all probability have so gone but for the outcry of the West, uttered at Chicago. It is yet to prove its right to be. It must do or die. Delegates can not, for any long period, be assembled triennially from the ends of this great land for the purpose of a mere dress parade. Clearly something must be done as well as talked about: and

so done as appreciably to influence coming events.
If the Council is to live permanently, it must realize and act up to the measure of its constitu-
tional duties. It must aid the churches in their
work. It is asked how that aid is to be rendered?
That is a question for the Council itself to answer.
It is to render the aid, and the how of it is left to
its own discretion. It must devise the ways and
means for itself. That is what it is for, and the
task imposed requires of it the active employment
of all the resources of consecrated statesmanship
at its command.''

This chapter must not be closed without a reference to his sympathy for the larger kingdom outside his own loved denomination. He desired the
union of Christendom, but not by the sacrifice of
principle. He longed for such an adjustment of
the missionary operations of all denominations as
that wasteful expenditure might be avoided, and
we might be spared the shame of seeing several
weak and struggling churches in a small com-
munity that could hardly well support one. One
of the best articles he ever wrote was a call for a
'' Congress of Denominations,'' primarily for the
purpose of righting this wrong, and learning how a
Christian statesmanship can be applied to this

question all over the land. We make an extended quotation from it, as it shows how deeply he felt the evil, as well as the keenness of his consciousness of denominational mistakes. He first quotes from the deliverance of the Boston Council on the subject: "That the division of such communities (communities of limited population) into several weak and jealous societies, holding the same common faith, is a sin against the unity of the body of Christ, and at once the shame and scandal of Christendom." Judge Currier says of it: "The declaration is grand and ringing, but who has heeded it? What has been *done* to abate the nuisance complained of? Nothing, nothing whatever, although seventeen stirring years have since borne their history to eternity. The fact is that no denomination can hope to grapple successfully with this giant evil that so afflicts and distracts small communities. The Congregationalists tried their hand at it faithfully and well and heroically for a hundred years, but came out of the struggle well nigh used up as a denomination. They were most self sacrificingly non-denominational in all directions, went into all union movements with a will, and furnished a good share of the piety, money and brains that were embraced in these enterprises. Good was doubtless done, for the Presbyterian body owes much of its present greatness to contributions of men and money from Congregational sources. This is so notorious that Congregationalism, as it existed prior to the last two or three decades, was well described as 'A stream that rises in New England, flows south and west and empties into Presbyterianism.' The Presbyterians are not to blame for this irrigating process. They are quite right in availing themselves of its benefits, for it not only enlarged the body, but greatly improved its quality. The only thing I blame them for is their graceless ingratitude for favors received. But what was the result of this self-sacrifice on the part of Congregationalists as tending in any appreciable degree to abate the odious nuisance we are denouncing? The outcome in that direction was nothing. The result upon the Congregationalists themselves as a denomination the statistics abundantly and painfully show. I say again that no one denomination, acting alone, can successfully wrestle with this monstrous evil. If the work is ever accomplished it will be achieved by the joint and concurring action of all.''

These are not the words of a man of sectarian spirit, but those of a far-seeing Christian statesman, who loved his own denomination, but who loved the great kingdom of Christ far more.

CHAPTER IV.

HIS AID TO INDIVIDUAL CHURCHES.

———

" We live in deeds, not years; in thoughts, not breaths;
In feelings, not in figures on a dial.
We should count time by heart throbs. He most lives
Who thinks most, feels the noblest, acts the best."

—*Bailey.*

CHAPTER IV.

HIS AID TO INDIVIDUAL CHURCHES.

Not long before his death, Lord Chesterfield wrote to his son: "I think of nothing now but how in the best way to kill time, since time is become my enemy. I have resolved to sleep in the carriage the rest of the journey." It was a ghastly admission of a wasted life, devoted to such pursuits as made no preparation for the days of weakness preceding the end. He lived a brilliant life, flattered by others, dazzling with the glory of this world. But no public services nor high official position under the king can cover the low moral tone of those letters that teach a refined selfishness smothered in wit and elegance. In startling contrast to this is the old age of the sincere Christian, whose years of service to the King of Kings have fitted him to still "bring forth fruit in old age." We do not think of such an one as old; the body fades and vanishes, but the helpful spirit lives, and even to the last the habit of beneficence is kept up, and when the end comes there are multitudes to rise up and call him blessed.

The main thought of the last years of the life of Judge Currier was that of doing good. He planned for it, deliberately studied how to accomplish the most good with the least outlay, in order that he might have left enough more with which to do further good. He made his personal expenses as small as was wise for one in his weak condition, and so used what was left of his annual income as to stimulate others to do their best. For many years he gave an average of $1000 a year to churches other than the one in which he was a member, and this was but a fraction of his beneficence. He recognized the fact that the blessing of God is and always has been on the organized church. He looked upon the running of a church as he would upon that of a business house, and believed that the same energy and discretion were needed in the one as in the other. It was his aim to teach young and struggling organizations this fact and show them the adaptation of means to ends. His was not a mystical faith that waits for miracles, but a practical belief that even God works better through the best appliances, and gives his seal of approval to those who consecrate

brain as well as heart to his service. This under-
lay all he did, and resulted while he lived in remarkable progress under difficulties, in widely
diverse localities, and the end is not yet—his work
is still being done, and will continue for ages.

One of the most fruitful acts of his life was in
connection with a fund that is now doing great
good in every part of the land. If he was not
the only one who knew the need he was the first
to make a practical offer that stirred up others to
meet the emergency. In the spring of 1886, Dr.
A. L. Frisbie, of Des Moines, Iowa, published in
the *Advance* an article entitled " Congregational
Constituencies," which attracted attention. It was
in the line of much of Judge Currier's thought,
and he immediately set about putting it in practical shape. In correspondence he offered to start a
loan fund for churches; he urged upon the Provisional Committee of the National Council, which
was to meet that fall in Chicago, the importance
of having the topic discussed, and suggested Dr.
Frisbie as the proper one to lead. To the secretary of the Church Building Society he made a
definite offer to be one of one hundred men to
give $1000 each, to constitute a fund to be loaned
to weak churches trying to build, and insisted that
the matter be taken up with vigor.

Dr. Frisbie's paper at the Council was entitled
" Churches on the Border Land of Self Support."
The results of the discussion were embodied in a
series of resolutions, concerning which Judge Currier had earnest correspondence in advance with
their author, calling for a " Church Loan Fund "
of $100,000, to be raised in large sums from indi-
viduals. In a personal letter Dr. Frisbie mentions
the Judge as promising the first $1000. The pro-
cess of securing that fund was as trying to the
energetic secretary of the American Congregational Union, now the Congregational Church
Building Society, as such efforts usually are. As
similar movements frequently do, it persistently
stuck at $85,000, and obstinately refused to move
farther. Judge Currier then wrote, proposing
that as an increase of twenty per cent in the
pledges would furnish more than the amount
needed, each one make that increase, and added
$200 to his own pledge. His whole subscription
of $1200 was paid in July, 1887. In a letter to
the Judge three years later, Secretary Cobb writes
as follows: "In a volume now open before me on
my table I have a list of donors and donations under this heading: 'The National Council Church
Loan Fund.' It foots up $102,960.62, plus ad-

ditions made by returns from the churches to which aid from this fund has been rendered. The total to-day is $114,415.21. This sum has been assigned to forty-three churches, in twenty-three states and territories. These churches, so far as I know, with one exception are doing well. One of them has paid back all it received. I am confident that most if not all the churches thus aided could not have prospered, even if they had lived, but for this timely aid. So much has come of your initial offer. You have this much of joy."

This represents a favorite mode of giving on the part of Judge Currier. He loved to stimulate others to do what without this stimulus must have remained undone. Many of his largest benefactions thus reduplicated themselves, and it would be difficult to enumerate the many channels by which strength was brought to dying churches. It also represents his belief that the true way to help all benevolent causes is to help the local church. Congregationalists have been ready to give in large sums for the Master's work, and the more undenominational the appeal the more hearty has been the response. In many places the word " Congregational " in connection with the appeal was a disadvantage; if it were a union matter it was sure of money. But there is a limit to that kind of giving. Members move away; givers die; the church that is wholly self-forgetful may awake to the consciousness that it has sacrificed a principle which was committed to its care. Others have profited by its liberality and grown strong at its expense, but at the sacrifice of its spirit. We have divine authority for mingling the wisdom of the serpent with the harmlessness of the dove. One must have a right hand if he is to use it. A wise beneficence will not only give for others, but will train up those of like spirit with itself to perpetuate the giving in coming years.

What if some narrow-minded people do cry out that it is sectarian! It is no more so than for the Christians of Macedonia to help those of Jerusalem, when it was really keeping alive the old Apostolic spirit. In our day the denomination that has been an inspiration to better life and grander sacrifice on the part of a dozen others can stand a little *esprit de corps* of a thoroughly Christian type. The college and the academy, the Sunday-School Union and the Bible Society, all merit assistance; but so does the little struggling church that only needs a lift over a hard place to make it the means of helping all these and many other good things in coming years. This was his belief, and it was a wise statesmanship looking to the future and planning to have larger things done then than now. One result of it is, that there are several churches in growing centers that are every year giving a large part of what they received into the various channels of benevolence, and swelling the stream of Christian helpfulness. Blessed is the man who sees this truth; the future will recognize the spirit that pervaded his life.

He believed in using the organized means of doing good, and his gifts to churches were either made through these channels or secured by wise provision so as to revert to them in case of the failure of the church. Yet he did much for individual enterprises; there was not a year in the latter part of his life when he did not put some church on its feet. Dr. Roy writes: "In his going south and west from year to year I know of his making it almost a passion to be looking out for the welfare of our churches, whether at Jacksonville, Fla., Atlanta, Ga., or in Colorado or Missouri. In his fighting for health he seems to have made it a pastime to be looking after the good of the churches as a business." The same story comes from every locality where he stopped for a time. The *Rocky Mountain Congregationalist* says: "We of Colorado have known his later life. We have known him for his active interest in all our pioneer home missionary work, and for his liberal and wisely-timed gifts to our churches when building, or getting out of the mire of debt."

His desire for church extension was shown early in the history of Pilgrim Church; we think it was a little before they had completed their chapel; it was a time when most churches would have thought it necessary to keep all their funds for their own need. An independent church had been organized out of the Biddle Market Mission Sunday-School; a lot had been purchased and a chapel erected, but not completed, at the corner of Sixteenth and Carr streets. One of the principal movers in the enterprise suddenly sickened and died. As a result of this death the leading members of the new church found themselves without funds to complete the building. Upon consultation they decided to offer the whole thing to the Congregationalists provided the latter would agree to pay the indebtedness and complete the building. The name of the church was to become Congregational. A meeting was called at Dr. Post's study, and the matter was carefully discussed. Mr. S. B.

Kellogg, then of the First Church, offered to make a personal pledge of $500. Judge Currier promised that Pilgrim Church should give one-half the amount needed provided the rest could be raised. Others who were consulted were not possessed of the daring of these two; the balance could not be raised, and so the project fell through. The Presbyterians gladly took the field and have worked it since.

One of the first organized churches in St. Louis to feel the impulse of the Judge's counsel and financial aid was the Third, when its location was such as to make growth impossible. His kind words and kinder deeds cheered the pastor to go forward and do what otherwise he had not dared to do. That pastor, Rev. Theodore Clifton, says: " In the first place I found the Judge's sympathy and friendship most helpful indeed in influencing Pilgrim Church friends to help us in our struggle to move from Boston Street to Francis Street, and for that work he gave us $75 in money, if I remember correctly. Then when it came to the struggle in buying the Grand Avenue lot he was grandly helpful in using his influence in Pilgrim Church on our behalf. He also gave $300 on that property." Years later, when the same church was trying to build its present attractive chapel, its pastor wrote to the judge for his counsel and such pledge as he felt like making. The response was sent by return mail, and illustrates his estimate of the value of concerted action as well as his love for and confidence in Pilgrim Church.

He wrote as follows: "I have considered the matter submitted to me in your note of the 9th inst., and reach this conclusion: if Pilgrim Church shall think well enough of your enterprise to aid it to the extent of $3,000, I am disposed to stand in for one-tenth of that sum, provided the whole transaction is consummated by the first day of April next. I put the matter in this way, since I wish herein to act under the leadership of the wise men of Pilgrim Church who are on the ground, and who can therefore judge much better than I what it may be best to do. I assume that they will look into the affairs of the Third Church and consider what it purposes to do and the importance of it, and the assurance for accomplishing the end in view without encumbering the property." Whenever it was possible he gave in this way, trusting to those whose judgment he knew to get at the facts, and making his own pledge conditioned on theirs. Pilgrim Church did look into this matter, approved it, and a handsome sum was raised, the Judge, as he had proposed, giving one-tenth. That church has now a property worth $30,000, the result of a helping hand at the right moment.

One of the best illustrations of his method is found in the Fifth, now the Compton Hill Church of St. Louis. It was situated in a neighborhood where the population shifted so rapidly that no church could long remain self-supporting. Yet it was doing a good work and seemed to have years of usefulness before it. Judge Currier had been one of the contributors to the fund for buying the property from an insurance company when another denomination failed there. He now wrote to the pastor, suggesting that no church could be permanently successful in any locality unless it was properly housed. The old frame chapel in which it was worshipping, inherited from a failure and associated with loss, was a hindrance to it. A correspondence followed, extending over several years, in which he first offered to help if the building enterprise was started; then he offered a definite sum on condition that work should begin within a year. Later, as his attention was called to a thrifty mission of the little church that was

itself nearly ready to be organized into a church.
he proposed to give $500 that year if the church
would build and at the same time the mission
would erect a modest chapel and begin church life.

The neighborhood about the church suddenly
began to change so rapidly that to move was the
only hope of keeping the organization alive. The
facts were written to the Judge, with the suggestion that the neighborhood of the mission was the
proper place for the church itself. By return mail
he sent a letter, withdrawing all former promises
of aid, and offering to give $1000 toward the pur-
chase of the new lot, on three conditions, of
which one was the approval of the move by the
Board of Deacons of Pilgrim Church, and another
was that the deed to the lot must be satisfactory
to himself. Three of the busiest weeks in the life
of that pastor were spent in meeting these conditions, with final success. The lot, costing $6500,
was bought, the Judge's check came promptly,
and the church that was then in danger of extinc-
tion now ranks third in the list of churches of the
Congregational household in that city in point of
strength, and second in membership. It was the
help over a hard place that did it; and when a year
later it was ready to build he followed up his other

investment with $300 more toward the building on conditions that led to the raising of $12,000 in all.

In many letters to those who were watching the trend of things in that city he said: "We must not only have many churches in St. Louis, but strong ones. It will be a mistake if we load ourselves only with enterprises that must always be helped." He looked over the field as a general might in the midst of the battle, and made up his mind what ought to be the next move. It is unusual to find a man outside the membership of a church urging that church to arise and build, and offering to give toward it more than any one of its members is likely to be able to give. One of his cherished hopes was that of seeing the two churches just mentioned comfortably housed in permanent buildings; he did live to see each in a fine chapel which will some day be part of a large and well equipped structure, but before he could help them take the next step God called him home.

In the same spirit he welcomed the steps taken by the "Congregational City Missionary Society of St. Louis" toward the occupancy of eligible locations in the rapidly growing western part of the city. Although absent, and seeing St. Louis but

once or twice a year, and then frequently unable
to leave his hotel, he kept well informed of its
rapid growth, and had definite ideas as to what
should be done. The region where the flourishing
Central Church now is early attracted attention,
and when he was informed of the project he was
ready to show his interest as in other localities,
and gave counsel and cash for making the proper
start.

Among the churches that cherish precious mem-
ories of his wisdom and beneficence none has more
reason to be grateful than the now successful
"Church of the Redeemer," at Atlanta, Ga. It
was in a critical condition, and its future seemed
uncertain, when he came to its aid. Rev. J.
Homer Parker, at one time its pastor, writes: "I
recall Judge Currier's presence in Atlanta when I
was pastor of the Church of the Redeemer, then
Piedmont. He was intensely interested in the success of that movement, which he considered the
key to the Congregational situation in the South.
He then and afterwards proved his interest not
alone by words of counsel, cheer and sympathy,
but also by contributing of his means. His faith
with that of others is bearing rich fruition."

As in other cases, he saw that the question of

continuing was all contained in that of building, and he counselled them strongly to move in the matter promptly and in force. But for the liberal sum contributed by himself, and the interest secured by him among friends in other cities, those most conversant with the history of that church are of the opinion that it would not have built, certainly not at the time it did. He corresponded with those he knew who might be able to help. He wrote to the officers of the Church Building Society. He himself gave liberally toward the purchase of the lot, and later for the erection of the chapel. His characteristic good judgment is shown in his letter to one of the secretaries of the American Home Missionary Society on this subject; we quote from it: "The thing to be done, and done speedily in my judgment, is to send a minister there who in ability and standing would rank favorably with the better class of ministers in Atlanta. Some such man as Dr. Eddy, whom I understand you have in view for that very work. In three months' time he would be able to get at the bottom and real inwardness of things there, and to advise you definitely and intelligently whether to go on with the work or abandon it. In some districts aid may be spun out though a series of years, but that policy will not work in Atlanta; what is done there must be done at the beginning to be effective. Once on their feet and respectably housed, the people there would take care of themselves and constitute a basis for further operations. If Atlanta is abandoned it will be useless to attempt work at any other point in the Southeast outside of Florida. The whole future of the Southeast, so far as we are concerned, hinges upon Atlanta.''

This was the deliberate judgment of a man who saw the whole field, who believed we have a mission to the white people of the South, and who had definite ideas as to how that mission should be fulfilled. Dr. Eddy did go to Atlanta; the church was comfortably, even elegantly housed; it has now a membership of over two hundred. It was in the right place to have a share in the reception of the large number of Congregational Methodist churches that turned to us later, and its pastor, Dr. Sherrill, has been able to exercise a very helpful influence on other movements because of the assured position of his church.

The feeling of this church was expressed in resolutions at the time of the dedication of its chapel, and after speaking of many of those who had rendered assistance, they closed as follows: "To every one who has aided us in any way, whether by prayer, influence or money, and especially to Judge Warren Currier, not only for the substantial aid he has so generously extended, but for coming to our relief in the darkest hours of our existence, when our flickering light was about to expire, making our condition known, and obtaining the cooperation of those able to help us; for his instrumentality in securing to us our beloved pastor, the Rev. Dr. Eddy, and for his continued sympathy, counsel and pecuniary aid at all times when needed."

He was too sick to be present at the dedication, but sent a letter to be read. As this was a turning point in the history of the denomination, it will not be out of place to give this letter in full:

"I am commissioned to convey to you the Christian salutations of Pilgrim Congregational Church, St. Louis. I congratulate you upon the inaugural ceremonies of this day, and upon the work they are fitted to commemorate. You have all wrought faithfully and well. I congratulate you upon the possession of a church site so beautiful for situation, so central, convenient and every way attractive, and upon the possession of a house of worship which has been appropriately described as a 'psalm of praise.' We congratulate you also and always upon the evidences we have of the Christian fellowship subsisting between you and other local bodies, of other names, in Atlanta. You appear to have been received with a generous, open-handed Christian courtesy that may well touch the heart of the patriot as well as the Christian. Pilgrim Church has observed all this, and with sentiments of high gratification. It may not be too much to say that the great North has observed it also. These things have not been done in a corner. They have been observed by a wide array of interested witnesses. And now may the Lord bless you all and keep you. May he make his face shine upon you, and be gracious unto you. The Lord lift up his countenance upon you, and give you and your people peace and prosperity in all this beautiful South land. In behalf of Pilgrim Church,

WARREN CURRIER, Messenger."

It would probably not be possible to make a complete list of the churches aided by him. A few, in addition to those already named, are those at Webster Groves and Hannibal, Mo.; four in Denver, and that at Greeley, Colo.; San Jose, Cal.; the Church of the Redeemer and the Hyde Park Church, St. Louis; that at Jacksonville, Fla.; a German church in Omaha; at least two other churches in South Florida. He was also of service to the Presbyterian Church in Marietta, Ga., during his stay there. Many others were blest by his benefactions and put in positions of strength through his aid wisely rendered. Many of his best gifts were so made that his name did not appear in connection with them. A favorite method was to propose to Pilgrim Church that a certain sum be given by it to the specified object, and his contribution would be anywhere from one-tenth to one-half of the whole amount. Few givers have made disposition of what they had to bestow with such care, and few have seen such great and varied results in their lifetime from their own careful investment of benevolent funds.

We can not better close this chapter than with a letter from Rev. Addison Blanchard, who was for several years a witness of his work for churches in Colorado. He writes as follows:

"I am glad to say a word about a man I respected and loved as I did Judge Currier. It is hard to say what one would like to in a few words of a man so unique. He was an enthusiast in his devotion to the principles of our Congregational churches, but he was never narrow, nor a selfish sectarian. He could not be. It was not in the make-up of the man. He loved Congregationalism for its absence of ecclesiastical rule and church courts and law. He saw in our way just that opportunity to do and to think under Christ in which every one who has come to know the freedom of the Gospel rejoices, when he understands his position. He was in the habit of studying our field and work in these western States. He knew and was ready to urge what was wise for us to undertake and how. He had an insight as to methods and missionary policy on the home field in the West which was remarkable. He advocated no policy which ignored the work of other churches. He always insisted that we should carefully understand what was our work, and spend our money for that alone. He insisted on a policy that would stand the test of years rather than on that which might appear well in the reports of any one year, or which might grace a single platform speech.

We shall miss his far-sighted opinions as to all forward movements in a home missionary way. To many who have felt the force of his wisdom this will be counted our greatest loss by his death.

"I met Judge Currier first in Denver, in 1882. He was always ready to hear anything I had to say about new work, and when he was fully convinced of the wisdom of the move was ready to give liberally. He gave with delight. He could always appreciate an emergency in a good cause, but you must show him that it was a good cause and a wise one. He gave in a way to stimulate others to do their best. When he doubted the policy of your new movement it was in vain to try to move him. Several important churches in Denver, as well as that at Greeley, have reason to remember his liberality in time of need."

CHAPTER V.

HIS LEGAL SERVICES.

———

"God is not a God of confusion, but of peace; as in all
the churches of the saints."

"Let all things be done decently and in order."

—*St. Paul, 1st Corinthians, 14: 33, 40.*

CHAPTER V.

The following estimate of him as a lawyer is given by one who was intimately associated with him for a time in the practice of his profession:

"Shortly after my acquaintance with the Honorable Warren Currier began he was elected to the office of Judge of the Supreme Court of the State of Missouri. At the time of his election he was a well-known and successful lawyer at, and a respected member of, the St. Louis bar. Many important questions, both of a public and private nature, came before the Court during the comparatively short time Judge Currier was a member of it; some of which grew out of the changes which followed the civil war. The court at that period comprised two other members, one of whom was the Honorable Philemon Bliss, the author of the valuable text book known as 'Bliss on Code Pleading;' he was afterwards an eminent instructor in the Law School connected with the State University at Columbia.

"As a Judge, Mr. Currier was upright, laborious and painstaking. Although thoroughly educated in the law, and well read, he never went out of his way to make a display of learning. He was a thoroughly practical man, and such were his opinions. They were simple and pure in style, clear and concise in statement, and eminently logical. The law was clearly stated and applied. This was very much at a time when the rapid accumulation of reports was becoming almost alarming.

"Judge Currier did not quite serve out his term. He had acquired a wide-spread reputation for integrity, and as being a man possessed of sound judgment in both legal and business affairs, and ability to grasp and deeply comprehend important matters, together with thoroughness and conservatism. He was a wise and safe counselor and adviser. Along with these went strong force of character and great tenacity of purpose in following out his resolves when once he was satisfied that he was right. It was not long before he was sought for to become the president of a large manufacturing establishment in the city of St. Louis. He accepted this offer, resigned his position on the bench, and remained with said establishment for some years, during which it transacted a prosperous business. Shortly after this he returned to the bar, but it was only a few weeks before he was taken down with an attack of acute illness, and his health became such that he was compelled to give up his purpose of again practicing law. If it had not been for this interruption his great and mature qualifications, combined with the confidence in himself which he inspired in others, would have brought him a large and valuable business."

The fact was that God had other plans for him. Those years of special preparation were not to be lost, but made the means of blessing to many thousands who had need of them, but knew not where to find them. The life that might have been one of the greatest ornaments to the legal profession, yet for many years was to be an honor to the church of God; and the busy brain that could have unravelled tangled questions of law was to have leisure to plan for the good of the Kingdom of the Redeemer. However great his services to the bar, his real greatness will always be in connection with Christian work, and the greatest accomplishments of his life were made after that life seemed to have been laid aside, and in the case of many another would have been forgotten.

Probably the churches do not know that they are indebted to Judge Currier for an excellent title to their property. This subject of titles has had too little attention, and we might have been spared some heavy losses in the past if the work of this careful man could have been done a few years earlier. Often the joy over a parcel of ground purchased at a great sacrifice blinds the members of a church to all other matters, and they leave the framing of a deed to some uninterested party, who intends to make the title good, but knows absolutely nothing about churches. A title drawn by such an one may be safe in law against all claimants from former ownership, while there is nothing to guard against loss under circumstances that have arisen many times in the past, and may at any time occur again. We sing with great enthusiasm,

> " When I can read my title clear
>   To mansions in the skies;"

there is a wise forethought in being able to read our title clear to earthly mansions, especially if they are set apart for the worship of God in accordance with the belief of a certain denomination. Money that is given for a Congregational Church should always be kept sacredly for the use of a Congregational Church and no other. If we expect to retain the confidence of men of large means, and to lead them to give generously for the erection of church edifices, we must be able to assure them that their gifts will be sacredly guarded in all coming time.

The parish system has not gained a very firm hold in the west, and as time passes the tendency becomes stronger to organize in such way that the church itself shall hold the property. In Missouri the law is such that it is possible to incorporate the church itself. Only two of the St. Louis churches now have societies, and they are the two that were organized first. All the younger ones are incorporated, or else their property is held in trust for them by the Congregational City Missionary Society until such time as they may become self-sustaining, when it will be transferred to them under the same form of trust deed as that under which it is now held.

One such lesson as we as a denomination received in the early part of this century ought to be sufficient to lead us to keep the title to all church property in the hands of those who are most likely to hold the church to the faith of Scripture. A Christian church ought to be able to attend to

its business, and the last vestige of the old union
of Church and State among people of our belief
should not have held on so long as it has.   Probably it would not have done so, but for the fear in
many of the churches that to take full charge of
their own affairs would alienate the strong men
who belonged to the society, and sheltered themselves under that fact, while their wives and
daughters were members of the church.   The
newer churches of the West have been free to do
the right thing because of their very newness, and
many of them have found their liberty in this regard.   Yet even with a Board of Trustees elected
by the membership of the church, and responsible
only to them, dangers frequently arise that can
only be averted by titles so arranged that the will
of those who purchased the property shall be carried out.

There is another danger, and Judge Currier was
prompt to see and guard against it: the peculiar
condition that has developed in the last few years
in connection with one of our seminaries illustrates
it.   A church or an institution should not be tied
irrevocably to old tradition nor to creeds that may
after a while be recognized as the excellent sym-
bols of a past generation, but as hardly expressing

the thought of the present. All this may take place without a particle of heresy being developed. Our denomination is a living, growing body; it is the only denomination in existence to-day that is thoroughly orthodox, and yet elastic. It firmly believes that John Robinson's famous words are true, and is so constituted that it can receive and assimilate all new truth that may break out of God's Word, and yet reject any so-called truth that breaks from somewhere else. The titles to church lots can certainly be trusted if they are so arranged as to take the property where the denomination goes, and nowhere else. To deny this is to put our work on the same plane with that of those churches that are anchored to the past, and intend to remain so anchored.

One of our greatest dangers, as shown by history, is from men of brilliant, popular gifts, who come into vacant pulpits, and sweep churches away as with a flood. These men may be sincere, but they are all the more dangerous as leaders. No one is likely to so utterly misguide a church as he who is unconsciously drifting in his thought, and whose drift gets into his preaching whether he will or no. Such a man may in a few years carry any church so far that it ceases to be in evangelical fellowship. Yet such a church will assert vehemently that because it has our polity it has a perfect right to call itself a Congregational Church. Congregationalism has stood in the past for a theology as well as a polity, and that theology has been a leavening influence in the thought of other denominations. Judge Currier believed that the theology and the polity are worth guarding.

A Unitarian church is frequently incorporated as the "First Congregational Society in ———;" but it is no more a Congregational Church than is a society for ethical culture. There are other churches as far away that claim to be Congregational, and cling to property whose deed specifies that it is for the uses of a Congregational Church, and no one seems able to dislodge them. The trouble is that the deed, while specifying a Congregational Church, does not define it.

Judge Currier gave careful thought to this subject in all its bearings for many years. The result is what able lawyers have admitted to be the best deed for Congregationalists yet devised. No one knows what some keen lawyer may do, but this seems to be safe so far as human language can make it. It has been changed but little since many years ago its author drew it for the Third

Congregational Church of St. Louis. We give it here for the use of any who may desire it. The portion not given is familiar to any lawyer, describing the property transferred, and giving properly the names of the parties to the transaction.

"In trust for the uses and purposes following, to-wit: For the sole use and benefit of the said grantee, the ——— Congregational Church of ———, a religious organization duly incorporated under the laws of the State of ———, to be occupied, held and used by it and its successors free of rent or other charge therefor as a place of religious worship and instruction and such other congruous uses as said church may desire, so long as the said church shall be an evangelical Congregational Church, associated with other Congregational churches represented in the National Council of Congregational Churches of the United States.

"In case said church shall be dissolved, or abandon the faith and ecclesiastical order recognized in said council as evangelical Congregational, then the title of said granted premises shall pass to and rest in the "Congregational Church Building Society," a corporation duly organized and ex-

isting by and under the laws of the State of New
York, in fee simple, to be held and disposed of by
it for the objects set forth in its charter, and it
shall be the duty of the trustees herein to make all
appropriate conveyance to carry into effect the
purposes herein contemplated.

"The grantee aforesaid is authorized to mortgage, sell and convey, in furtherance of the trust
above stated, the said premises in such way and
manner as the said church may authorize and direct; such authorization and direction being shown
by the vote of said church at a meeting thereof
duly called and held for that purpose, and passed
by a majority of all the adult male members of
said church present at such meeting."*

---

*NOTE.—The deed as given above is as Judge Currier
drew it. The following clauses are now added, and are here
given for the sake of any who may desire to use the form.
Beginning from the words "present at such meeting," the
new portion reads: "but the proceeds of such mortgage or
sale shall be used only for the trust herein above named, and
in case of an attempt to use them otherwise such proceeds
shall at once revert as above. It shall not, however, be the
duty of the purchaser or purchasers, mortgagee or mort-
gagees, to see to the application of the proceeds of such sale,
sales, mortgage or mortgages, nor shall any misapplication
of such proceeds by the grantee herein in any manner affect
the validity of any such conveyance or mortgage."

The deed here given is now used regularly by the Congregational City Missionary Society of St. Louis, and all its property is held under it. Judge Currier, in the original deed, specified by name the trustees to whom the conveyance was made, stating that they are the trustees of said church, and that their successors shall be the trustees elected from time to time by said church.

Several things are accomplished by this deed, and were intended to be so accomplished by its framer. First, and most important, no one who reads it can for a moment doubt what is intended by the term "Congregational Church." For all the purposes for which this property is to be used it can only be one of the kind described in the deed. Others may make claims for themselves and write names in their deeds, but it is perfectly plain that the intent of this conveyance is, that the church that holds the property shall not be an independent church. It must be associated with other Congregational churches. Nor is it enough that it be in some Association that calls itself Congregational; that Association must be represented in the National Council. Who that intends to have things done decently and in order can ever find fault with this? "If we are Congregationalists at all let us be thorough ones," said the Judge one day.   There is nothing to be gained by a half-way position.   If one of us goes into Presbyterianism or Methodism he has to go in all over; why not do the same in Congregationalism? and why not ask the same of those who come to us?   They will respect us more for doing so.

But making a church thoroughly Congregational means that it shall have the power of expansion. Liberty of thought within evangelical lines and the right to follow the leadings of one's own conscience have always been cardinal principles with us.   We have erred sometimes in our application of them, and have blundered into other ways of doing things than that we purposed.   We have also inherited organizations that were not intended to be Congregational, and so were not formed in line with these principles.   But we are living in an age when true Congregationalists are looking about to find in what way we are at variance with ourselves, and the present unrest in many quarters means a final readjustment on lines that shall be recognized as consistent.   We must not be too closely tied to the past, however excellent it is; so the Judge in framing this deed said to those whom he consulted that the National Council, whatever changes may come to it, will represent the true status of Congregationalists in any given age, and property that goes theologically where the National Council goes may be regarded as safe for the uses of a Congregational Church for all time. He had unbounded faith in the underlying sincerity and good sense of our kind of Christians, and was willing to trust the men of the future to take care of the orthodoxy of the future. Would that there were more than there are of like faith and practice.

Again, he believed that money given for Congregational uses is a sacred trust, and must always be kept for those uses and no other. He recognized the right of a church to change its polity, but not thereby to alienate the gifts of those who in the past have seen the struggles of God's people, and out of sympathetic hearts and with much consecration have given of their substance to help perpetuate the principles which those struggling Christians represented. A reversionary clause like that in the deed has in some instances proved a great help in strengthening a wavering theology. If it be objected that this does not seem a high motive for holding the truth, it must be replied that neither is the motive always high that leads a man to depart from the old standards, and ally himself with those who do not keep a Scriptural faith. It is well to do right even toward the dead, and if one's departure from the faith is sincere he will be willing to do for it what they did who founded and made strong the church from which he departs.

Fortunately we have an organization whose charter makes it a natural custodian of certain classes of trust funds. Our Church Building Society is, and ought to be, able to take care of any property that may revert to it by reason of the death of a church or its change of faith and polity. It is constantly doing so, and doing it well. The real estate of some of the most thrifty churches we now call Congregational is held by such deeds as the above, and would immediately revert to the Church Building Society in case of any change. Judge Currier believed in that Society, and regarded the trust clause as of the greatest importance. The society is the friend of the church, and can only have a legal interest in the property when the church ceases to be what it was meant to be. The property can be mortgaged or sold, provided the original intent is carried out in so doing. The only object of the trust clause is to prevent the perversion of funds.

Another matter which received his special attention is the manner in which church property may be wisely transferred. He had a great horror of the vote of a meeting of uninformed, irresponsible young people, when the action referred to legal or money interests. He believed that the business matters of a church should have the most careful attention of the most thoughtful members. For this reason he limits the voting power for the transfer of real estate to those who are most likely to be informed on that subject, the business men of the church, whose daily life makes them careful of property interests.

The constitutions of the churches are as various as the churches themselves; the franchise in some is limited to men, in others to all members over a certain age, and cases have been known where a church was so careless of its own interests as to permit those not in its membership to vote at its business meetings. We allow the freedom of the will to churches as well as to individuals, and rightly; but real estate purchased by the self-sacrifice of large-hearted friends is too sacred to be voted away in some moment of anger or excitement, and there is no danger of guarding it too carefully.

For this reason he made the deed such that, in order to transfer the property and give a clear title, it is necessary that a meeting for that purpose shall be called, due notice being given; at that meeting the vote that makes the transfer must be a majority of two-thirds of the adult male members of that church who are present at that meeting. The church may be careless in other matters if it choose; but no lawyer who understands his business is likely to let it evade the provision in its deed that must be met in order to give a clear title.

Few deeds accomplish so much in so few words as does this one; and if its insertion here should lead to its more general adoption by young churches it may serve as a bond to still further unite us in a common faith and practice. There is no power to compel its adoption; it must stand by reason of the good sense there is in it. In time, with the new problems that arise, some other form may prove more desirable; but we have good authority for saying, that at present there is no better known means for protecting the interests of the churches and the gifts both of the living and the dead. Judge Currier himself made it one of the conditions of his giving to churches that their title must be satisfactory to himself, which usually meant the adoption of his deed if the property was being purchased. As the number of large givers increases, the importance of these matters becomes more manifest, and benefactors are exercising greater care than ever before to see that their interests are protected. It is their right, and no church has any business to come before the public and ask for help unless it can show that the money so raised will be sacredly guarded for the purpose for which it was given.

We have aimed to give the story of this unusually helpful life in such manner that it may still be of use to those who read. Few men make so lasting an impression on church life, and few show such remarkable adaptability to the times in which they live. He dealt with real problems, and he showed great impatience in his later years with those who waste the present in fruitless discussion on topics that, to say the least, are unessential. He saw the opportunities in the field, and tried to lead

others to see and use them.   The great acts of his
life are all of them the result of his habit of careful attention to details, and the same qualities that
made him a good lawyer, a just judge, and a successful business man, made him a shaper of events
in the church.   His wisdom will appear more and
more as time shows the necessity for the measures
he championed.   We are drawing closer together
as Christian workers, and the results of his years
of painful study are all such as help in practical
work.   Let us note in closing how much he added
to the stock of usable power among Congregational Christians.

He originated the National Council.   He watched
carefully its development, and exercised great influence upon those who have so far made it a success, suggesting many of the themes that have
proved most fruitful, and above all insisting that
it must be a working body, and not a mere expression of good fellowship, as some would have made
it.

He was the first giver toward, and in that sense
the originator of, the National Council Exigency
Loan Fund, of upwards of $100,000, which is
proving a boon of inestimable value to hundreds
of weak and struggling churches all over the land.

He put life and hope into not less than
thirty churches in all parts of the country, and
in various stages of discouragement, so that they
determined to push forward and become worthy
of the respect of men and the blessing of
God. This he did with counsel, with money from
his own purse, and by persistent efforts he en-
listed the sympathy of others, so that many thousands of dollars were given for this purpose and
the stream of beneficence was greatly enlarged.

While doing this he was thoughtful of the future, in the interest both of givers and receivers,
and framed the deed that, so far as human
language is capable of it, guards against the diver-
sion of such funds from their proper use.

All this was done in the firm belief that Congregational Christianity, with its noble past, has a
yet more noble future, and only needs to be thoroughly united for aggressive work in the name of
the Master to prove itself to be not only the
nearest in its polity to the church of the New Tes-
tament, but the one that is most capable of receiving and using the gift of the Holy Spirit. If this
is sectarianism, it is of a kind that can be held
without detriment to love for all the church of
God everywhere, and is much needed now for the

development of the mighty reserved forces which,
unless all the signs of the times are misleading,
are about to be called into play in the great climax
of the church on earth.